The Jacket

Sue-Ellen Pashley

illustrated by Thea Baker

WALKER BOOKS
AND SUBSIDIARIES

LONDON • BOSTON • SYDNEY • AUCKLAND

The jacket was no ordinary jacket.

It was soft, like dandelion fluff.

It was warm, like the afternoon sun.

It was comforting, like a hug

from your favourite teddy.

And it had four dazzling buttons

down the front.

The jacket went home with Amelia.

She wore it everywhere.

She wore it to nursery.

And to Aunty Kath's house.

And to the shops.

And to bed.

Until, one day, she couldn't

fit into it anymore.

So Mum suggested she give

it to Lily.

Lily wore it everywhere.

She wore it to the park.

And to Nana's house.

And to the library.

And to the beach.

Until, one day …

she couldn't fit into it anymore either.

So Lily put the jacket

on her favourite doll.

Lily and her doll had tea together.

And played in the sandpit.

And jumped on the trampoline.

Until Lily grew big

and went to school …

and stopped playing with her doll.

The jacket didn't seem so special anymore.

It was still soft and warm and comforting,

but now it had paint on the elbow.

And dirt on the hem.

And threads coming loose at the collar.

And only three dazzling buttons down the front.

The jacket was left in the corner of Lily's room,

half hidden under the wardrobe.

No longer going to the park.

Or to Nana's house.

Or to nursery. Or to bed.

Until one day, Cornflake the cat had kittens.

They curled up on the jacket.

They were five of the softest, warmest,

most beautiful things that Lily had ever seen.

She curled the jacket around them and it held them and kept them warm. And when the kittens were bigger, they went to their new homes.

Mum picked up the jacket.

She looked at its painted elbow.

And its dirty hem.

And its thread pulled collar.

And the cat fur that covered it.
And said, "We should get rid
of this old, dirty thing."

Lily was sad.

Was her jacket an old, dirty thing?

Even with its two remaining

dazzling buttons?

She thought of when she'd

worn it to the beach.

And Nana's house.

And the shops.

And to bed.

And how it had held the kittens.

Mum was very clever.

She measured and cut and sewed

until…

The teddy was

no ordinary teddy.

It was soft, like dandelion fluff.

It was warm, like the afternoon sun.

It was comforting,

like wearing your favourite jacket.

And it had two dazzling buttons

down its front.

For Jack, Gabby and Lawson —
who dream and imagine in so many
different ways — and are happy
to let me dream and imagine.
Love you with all my heart, always.

S.P.

For Zuri,
no ordinary girl;
love you more than
a thousand stars.

T.B.

First published in Great Britain 2019
by Walker Books Ltd
87 Vauxhall Walk,
London SE11 5HJ

10 9 8 7 6 5 4 3 2 1

Text © 2019 Sue-Ellen Pashley
Illustrations © 2019 Thea Baker

The right of Sue-Ellen Pashley and Thea Baker to be
identified as the author and illustrator respectively of
this work has been asserted by them in accordance
with the Copyright, Designs and Patents Act 1988

This book has been typeset in Cochin

Printed in China

British Library Cataloguing in Publication Data: a catalogue
record for this book is available from the British Library

ISBN 978-1-4063-8870-1

www.walker.co.uk